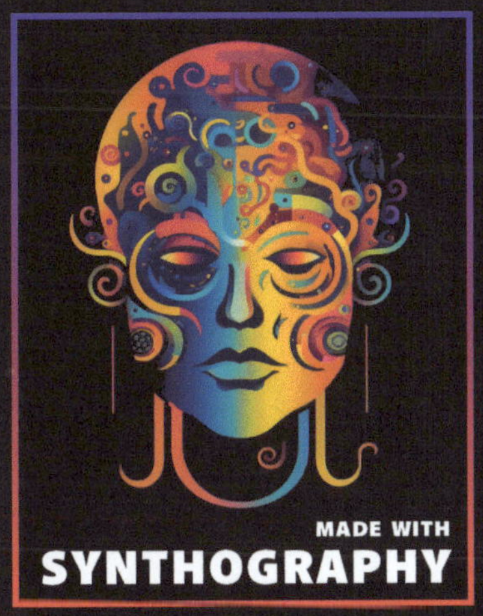

Oh Hey
VOID!

THE FOLLOWING MATERIAL MAY NOT BE SUITABLE FOR CHILDREN
UNDER THE AGE OF 17. THIS PROJECT CONTAINS VIOLENCE,
EXPLICIT LANGUAGE, AND GORE.

THE FOLLOWING MATERIAL WAS WRITTEN BY HUMAN WRITERS.
SOME CLARIFYING WORDING WAS EDITED BY MACHINE LEARNING TOOLS.
IMAGES IN THIS PROJECT WERE CREATED USING 3D DESIGN, PHOTOBASHING,
COMPUTER GENERATED IMAGERY, AND SYNTHOGRAPHY.

NO ARTIST STYLES WERE PROMPTED
DURING THE SYNTHO OR WRITING PROCESS.

FOR MORE INFORMATION VISIT
WWW.OHHEYVOID.COM

Oh Hey
VOID!

www.ohheyvoid.com
Copyright © 2024 Oh Hey Void

Paperback:978-1-957305-11-0
Ebook:978-1-957305-12-7

Written by Amber R Wilkinson & Jayson Wall
Edited by Rolayne Martin

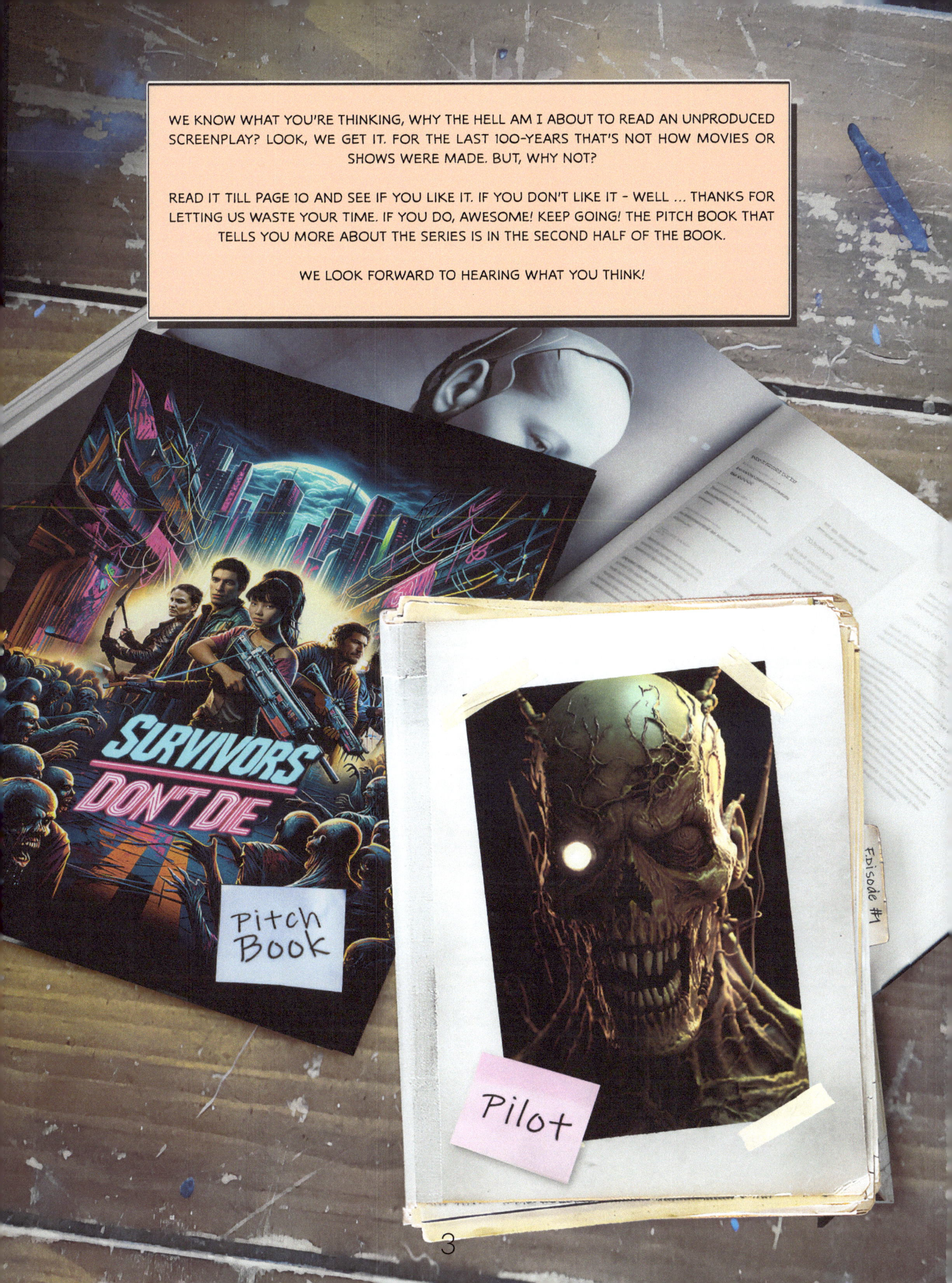

WE KNOW WHAT YOU'RE THINKING, WHY THE HELL AM I ABOUT TO READ AN UNPRODUCED SCREENPLAY? LOOK, WE GET IT. FOR THE LAST 100-YEARS THAT'S NOT HOW MOVIES OR SHOWS WERE MADE. BUT, WHY NOT?

READ IT TILL PAGE 10 AND SEE IF YOU LIKE IT. IF YOU DON'T LIKE IT - WELL … THANKS FOR LETTING US WASTE YOUR TIME. IF YOU DO, AWESOME! KEEP GOING! THE PITCH BOOK THAT TELLS YOU MORE ABOUT THE SERIES IS IN THE SECOND HALF OF THE BOOK.

WE LOOK FORWARD TO HEARING WHAT YOU THINK!

EPISODE LOGLINE
A band of survivors, determined to rescue others, finds themselves ensnared by a zombie horde, only to be swept into the deceptive safety of a cult-like sanctuary, where salvation hides sinister secrets.

SURVIVORS DON'T DIE

EPISODE 1

"Introduction"

written by

Amber Wilkinson
&
Jayson Wall

<u>ACT 1</u>

1   **EXT. NUVITTA SKYLINE - SUNSET**

        A futuristic city of curved buildings and roof top gardens
        buzz with the sound of drones flying overhead. Emergency
        sirens blaring in the distance.

2   **EXT. DARKYARD STREET - SUNSET**

        People are moving through the street with confusion. Many are
        glued to their wrist-units.

        A MAN with a bionic arm is crossing the street. He is viewing
        a holographic alert on his palm that reads, "SEEK COVER
        IMMEDIATELY"

        Behind him is GENJI RUSSO, 17. He has a tight hold on his
        sister, YUKI RUSSO, 11, as they move through the crowded
        cross walk.

        Yuki's wrist unit is projecting news footage of a convenience
        store in flames on the palm of her hand.

                        YUKI
                I'm telling you, it was one of
                those drones finally crashing. Now
                people are looting or something...

                        GENJI
                Whatever it was, we need to get off
                the street.

                        YUKI
                You're overreacting. If anything we
                should go check it out--

        BOOOM! An explosion errupts from one of the fancy high rises
        a few blocks down.

                        GENJI
                That's not a drone.

        Yuki holds up her hand to the smoke billowing into the sky.
        She makes a hand gesture and her wrist unit zooms in. Bodies
        plummet from the opening in the building.

                        YUKI
                What...is that?

        A SCARED MAN runs frantically passed them. A series of
        screams echo up the street.

More people start rushing by. Genji takes firm hold of Yuki's coat and pulls her as he picks up pace away from the explosion.

                    YUKI (CONT'D)
          Genji, stop! Stop!

                    GENJI
          Come on!

Genji looks back to witness A BUSINESS MAN with frantic movement yanking a WOMAN by the hair. She falls to the ground and TWO PEOPLE join the man in feasting on her.

Genji's attention turns in time to spot a BLOODY MAN reaching out for Yuki.

YUKI SCREAMS!

                    BLOODY MAN
          HELP ME! YOU HAVE TO HELP ME!

The man is holding a large wound at the base of his neck.

Without hesitation, Genji grabs the man and shoves him away.

                    GENJI
          HEY! FUCK OFF, MAN!

The Bloody Man smacks his head on the corner of the building. His body goes limp at the edge of an alley.

Genji and Yuki freeze at the site of the man's lifeless form.

                    YUKI
          Oh, shit.

                    GENJI
          Fuck-fuck--fuuck! Hey sir!?

Genji kneels down as more people rush by. The man's eyes are lifeless as he looks through the two teens.

                    GENJI (CONT'D)
          I think he's dead.

THEY JUMP! The Bloody Man begins to convulse on the ground.

Genji rolls the man on his side.

Black and red veins jolt up into the man's face and eyes.

Without warning he **_BITES DOWN_** on Genji's arm!

The boy **YELLS OUT** and begins punching frantically. After a few blows the Bloody Man lets go, but changes tactics. He chomps at Genji's face.

The two tussle for a brief moment, until Genji is able to free a large switchblade from his boot.

The sharp blade makes contact with the Bloody Man's ear. His body slumps to the ground.

Catching his breath, Genji stands up in a hurry.

Yuki is off to the side wide-eyed and shocked. Eyes glued to the body.

Genji takes Yuki's hand and pulls her back onto the street.

3   **INT. RUSSO APARTMENT - CONTINUOUS**

The front door of a high end apartment swings open and Yuki enters first. Further down the hallway is Genji, struggling to keep pace.

                    YUKI
          Genji! Hurry Up!

The boy's free hand clutches at his arm, blood dripping with every step despite a make shift tourniquet. His breathing heavy as he slams the door behind them.

Yuki sets up the security system. The keypad reads, "Lockdown Protocol Initiated."

The sound of heavy locks engage inside the door.

Genji's knees buckle and he slides against the wall to the ground. His breathing haggard.

Yuki quickly joins him.

                    YUKI (CONT'D)
          What do I do? I don't know what to
          do.

                    GENJI
          Take this.

Genji forces the blade into Yuki's hand.

                    YUKI
          No. No. NO... I can't-- I can't do
          that. I can't do that--

                    GENJI
          Okay. Okay. Okay Yuki! Okay, just
          breathe. Breathe...

His grasp tightens on hers, keeping her from pulling away.

Genji takes in a deep shaky breaths. Yuki mirrors him with
calmer inhales. The siblings calm down for a brief moment.

                    GENJI (CONT'D)
          I can't stop the bleeding. If I
          pass out, you take this and you--

                    YUKI
          No. You're going to be okay. Mom
          and Dad'll get here. You'll be
          okay...

                    GENJI
          But if I'm not- you hide. You
          protect yourself. Okay?

Yuki cries as her hand trembles.

The boy closes his eyes as he swallows. His skin pale.

                    YUKI
          No. No. Wake up!

Genji opens his eyes, but is visibly fading.

His eyes roll in the back of his head. And something deep
inside him causes his body to jerk!

Yuki half heartedly points the switchblade at her brother,
her tears hysterical.

Genji's shoulder shakes uncontrollably.

Yuki's eyes widen as she watches veins of black and red creep
up his neck.

The boy's entire chest cavity convulses.

                    YUKI (CONT'D)
          ...Genji... please...

SUDDENLY, HE GRABS HER! HE JERKS HER CLOSER. THE LARGE SWITCH
BLADE BETWEEN THEM.

BLACK AND RED VEINS TRAVEL UP HIS FACE AND INTO HIS EYES.

GENJI'S JAW LUNGES FORWARD TO BITE AS HE FORCES YUKI'S HAND.

Include flashes of
this scene in
Audit Episode

CRREAEESSSHHHH!!!

THE BLADE JERKS UPWARD INTO HIS THROAT.

His grip loosens on her shirt. The girl stands up quickly, her hands covered in blood.

Dropping the blade at her brother's feet Yuki backs away.

BANG! BANG! BANG!

The door violently shakes. The doorknob jiggles.

Yuki's entire body trembles in shock as she stares at the door, terrified.

BANG! BANG! A *RINGING* fills Yuki's ears as the door bows from the sheer force pushing its way in. Yuki can't hear anything through the high pitched sound of shock as she stares at Genji's body.

The doorframe cracks. Then it swings forcefully open.

TIM, a tall lanky 20-something enters the room. He glances at Genji's body and without hesitation gets eye level with Yuki.

Her eyes are wide and glazed over, her body trembling.

                    TIM
            (muffled)
      We need to get out of here, Yuki.
      Are you okay? You're gonna be okay.

The ringing in Yuki's ears intensifies.

4   **EXT. OUTSIDE RUSSO APARTMENT WINDOW - CONTINUOUS**

Through the window, we see Tim pull Yuki out the front door.

The city of Nuvitta is in chaos. Smoke billows out of high-tech organic skyscrapers as police drones fly overhead.

Tim and Yuki join the other survivors as they take to the streets to escape the carnage.

The last remnants of sunset dip down along the city horizon line. The pink and yellow tones of the sky disappear into the darkness.

<u>END ACT 1</u>

<u>ACT 2</u>

5   **EXT. ANTENNA ROOFTOP - MORNING**

SUPER: TWO YEARS LATER

The Nuvitta skyline glistens against a blue sky. Elegant
structures share the space with organic rooftop gardens and
city foliage below.

Birds fly freely between the buildings.

It's a peaceful, tranquil morning.

Clink--Clink--Clink!

YUKI RUSSO, now a resourceful and determined 13-year-old, is
pounding a wrench against a utility box.

                    YUKI
               (muttering)
          Come on, you stubborn piece of...

Before she can finish her swing, TIM grabs her arm and
snatches the wrench from her.

                    TIM
          Shh! Are you out of your mind?

                    YUKI
          How else am I gonna-

Tim rotates the wrench and pushes a button activating a green
laser.

                    YUKI (CONT'D)
          --Oh. Right.

Grabbing the laser back, Yuki cuts the lock with quiet
precision.

Inside the utility box is a digital touch screen. Tim quickly
plugs his WRIST UNIT into the available ports.

                    TIM
               (yelling to Oli)
          Alright, Oli! We're in.

OLI, a skilled and seasoned woman in her 40's, stands near a
large metal crate.

She pulls on an orange strap. The top of the crate flies open
as a sleek METAL FLOWER mechanically rises.

Network
Solar
Source

Network
Building #2

Bunker
Rooftop

Its petals made of solar panels turn towards the sun. Small
indication lights begin to blink on each stem.

Tim opens his palm. His wrist unit projects a hologram
against his fingertips.

The words "CONNECTED... BOOSTING SIGNAL..." appear.

                    YUKI
          How long will it take before anyone
          sees?

                    TIM
          Not sure.

Oli, satisfied with their work, begins to climb down a
ladder.

                    OLI
          Are we good?

                    TIM
          Uh, yeah. We'll have to wait it out
          back at base.

                    OLI
          Good, let's head back before
          morning rush.

Tim unplugs his device. And the trio head towards the roof
access door.

                    YUKI
          What if it doesn't work?

                    TIM
          Hey! Don't jinx it.

As they exit, the antenna on top of the building blinks a
blue light high over the city.

6   **EXT. STREET TO BUNKER - DAY**

A narrow one-way street is cleared of all debris. Windows and
doors are boarded up. Graffiti decorates the walls.

A five-story building protected by a shipping container wall
deadends the street.

The lettering on the building reads, "Network Building #2."

                    TIM
          Hard to tell, but it's out there.
          Now we wait.

Ji leans into the doorway of the server room. Wiping ash off
his face with a rag.

                    JI
          I'm tellin' ya, we don't need
          nobody knowin' we're here.

                    TIM
          We've already voted on this one,
          Ji.

                    YUKI
          You lost.

                    JI
          I know. I just don't think you
          people are listening.

                    YUKI
          Ugh! Go be a bad vibe somewhere
          else.

A speaker crackles on with Oli's voice.

                    OLI (O.S)
          As exciting as this morning's run
          was, we still got chores, and now a
          horde cleanup, people. Move in ten.

The three frown at the order.

Ji saunters down the hallway. Tim and Yuki mock him in
amusement.

14   **INT. INDOOR GARDEN - DAY**

The garden is a wide-open office space lined with rows of
plants. Hydroponic pipes of grapes, strawberries, herbs, and
flowers hang from the ceiling. Raised beds filled with rich
soil flourish with vegetables.

Above are large solar lamps letting off ample light.

Zola takes soil samples from one of the beds when the light
above him flickers.

                    ZOLA
          Don't die... don't die...

The light goes out. The man lets out a groan. Stepping up on a stool, he gets high enough to give the light a firm smack with his palm.

It flickers back on.

Oli enters with a water filter unit in hand as Zola climbs down from the stool.

> OLI
> Any spare water filters?

> ZOLA
> Lockers.

Oli makes her way to a row of lockers on the far wall. Each door is digitally labeled with supplies and low quantity counts. A number of the digital screens have big red X's on them. They indicate there are no more.

Opening the locker that reads, "Filters | QTY 1," Oli begins a search. She throws out multiple empty boxes until she finds a filter.

> OLI
> Last one.

> ZOLA
> We'll be okay. Someone will see it.

> OLI
> Well, we got 90 days to figure it
> out or we're fucked.

She leaves. Zola looks around the garden.

> ZOLA
> (to the plants)
> Don't listen to her. We'll be fine.

15   **INT. INDOOR BARN - DAY**

An office floor has been fashioned into an indoor stable. Three dairy cows MOO in greeting from a grassy section of the space. Yuki pats them on their heads as she turn on a feed-bot. The mechanical worker fills a trough with pellets.

Goats bleat as she scoops pellets from the trough. She tosses the feed on the ground.

The sound of a forklift *BEEPS* outside. Yuki opens one of the office windows to get a better look down below.

16   **EXT. STREET TO BUNKER - CONTINUOUS**

Ji backs up a forklift stacked with charred zombie bodies
down the street.

Tim is reloading the air cannons of the security system.

Tim stops his task to examine a glowing red and white
mushroom. He carefully picks the mushroom and places it in
his pocket. Glancing around to make sure no one saw.

17   **EXT. BUNKER ROOFTOP - CONTINUOUS**

Zola and Oli are peering down the scopes of their crossbows
keeping a close eye on Tim and Ji's surroundings below.

                        ZOLA
            What happened this morning?

                        OLI
            Horde moved into our path. Had to
            go through.

                        ZOLA
            That's not good news.

                        OLI
            Nope.

                        ZOLA
            Should we ... think about
            relocating?

                        OLI
            To where?

                        ZOLA
            I don't know...but if they're
            creeping out this way we need to
            consider our options, right?

                        OLI
            Let's stick to one plan at a time,
            yeah? We try this rescue outreach,
            find some others, then...we'll do
            some neighborhood cleanup once we
            have more manpower.

                        ZOLA
            What if they don't come?

                        OLI
            Then we figure it out. Always do.

A zombie wanders into Oli's sight line just behind Ji's forklift. She releases her arrow and **SPLAT!** Headshot.

18   **INT. BUNKER NETWORK ROOM - DUSK**

Tim's message continues to float in the hologram display.

"Hello? Can anyone see this?"

Yuki walks past the open door with a basket of eggs and mason jars full of milk.

She peeks into the room. She lets out a scoff of dissapointment when she realizes no one has responded.

19   **INT. BUNKER KITCHEN - DUSK**

Yuki enters an industrial-style kitchen with chrome countertops, stoves, and fridges. Crates of rations are stacked in the corners.

Ji enters, freshly showered. He reaches for his apron and begins going through Yuki's basket.

                    JI
          How many we get this time?

                    YUKI
          Five.

                    JI
          That's enough to make an omelet.

Yuki hands him the five chicken eggs.

                    YUKI
          They need better feed. Maybe, when
          we get more people we can loot that
          feed store again.

                    JI
          More people doesn't always mean
          better, kid.

                    YUKI
          Why are you so anti-social? It's
          boring.

Ji mocks her. Yuki starts gathering plates and silverware to make the table. Ji prepares to make dinner.

                    YUKI (CONT'D)
          You really don't think it'll work?

                    JI
          Look. Two years in a hostile
          environment makes people dangerous.
          We don't know what kind of people
          survived out there.

                    YUKI
          We survived.

                    JI
          No, we got lucky.

                    YUKI
          But, other people can be lucky too.

                    JI
          Yeah, but they can also be a big
          problem for us if they decide they
          want our luck for themselves.

                    YUKI
          We'd be saving them. Wouldn't most
          people be happy about that?

                    JI
          Sure. But some folks don't know how
          to regulate a win. They keep asking
          for more, and more and when they
          can't get any more, they can do
          some stupid shit.

                    YUKI
          Mmm... I'm gonna believe the ones
          we find won't be like you.

                    JI
               (mocking)
          Mmm... Probably a good idea.

20   **INT. BUNKER NETWORK ROOM - NIGHT**

Yuki and Tim are getting ready for bed. Tim is settling into
his hammock, while Yuki is staring intently at the lingering
message from her cot;

"Hello? Can anyone see this?"

                    TIM
          Hey... It's gonna work.

                    YUKI
          Yeah, it has to.

She reaches over and turns out the light between them. They
settle into the glow of the hologram.

21   **INT. NETWORK ROOM - LATER THAT NIGHT**

The room is dimly lit, and the Nuvitta Network Console casts
a faint light across the space.

Tim is asleep in his hammock, his wrist unit plugged into the
wall.

Yuki is asleep, her blankets kicked to the floor and her arm
dangling over the cot.

The clock reads 4:57am.

The message floats alone, *"Hello? Can anyone see this?"*

Suddenly, an active ellipsis appears as someone types in the
network chat.

A message appears, *"ROSIE596: Hello? Yes, I can see this. Are
you there?"*

22   **INT. NETWORK ROOM - MORNING**

The room is bathed in soft morning light from the diffused
newspaper-covered windows.

Tim yawns and stretches his arms. His hammock gently sways
beneath him.

He rubs his face and sniffs, trying to shake off the remnants
of sleep as he sits up and glances toward the console.

His eyes widen when he notices the response. He bolts out of
the hammock and stumbles toward his chair. His eyes scan the
message.

His hands shake, and his fingers begin typing on the
keyboard.

He sends, 'Here. *Where are you?*'

The active ellipsis appears. Tim gleefully claps his hands.

                    TIM
          Yes! Fucking yes!!!

Yuki bolts upright still waking up.

                    YUKI
          ...What?

                    TIM
          We got one.

                    <u>END ACT 2</u>

<u>ACT 3</u>

23   **EXT. BUNKER COURTYARD - MORNING**

The courtyard between Network Building #2 and the shipping
container wall is a circular driveway. The windows of the
building are boarded up. Wooden crates are used as flower
beds while heavy military artillery is organized nearby.

The five-person crew is strapping on the last of their travel
gear.

Tim presses a button on his futuristic javelin. It retracts
into a baton-shaped hilt.

Yuki finishes strapping her hunting slingshot to her wrist.
Extending it and retracting it for good measure.

Oli tosses Zola a resin capsule that he locks into his
futuristic bow quiver. He retrieves an arrow that rapidly 3D
prints itself so they never run out of ammo.

Ji is smoking a hand-rolled cigarette in the doorway, his
billhook strapped to his chest. He places his metal cigarette
case into his vest pockets and joins the team.

                    JI
          Before we all go and get ourselves
          killed. I wanna re-vote.

          OLI   YUKI
What the fuck is wrong with   Come on, we're already
you?   outside.

                    TIM
          Why do you always have to do this,
          man?

                    JI
          Don't you think we need more info
          before we go halfway across town
          for some stranger?

                    OLI
          Ji! We're running out of supplies.
          We don't have enough people to do a
          provisions recon. And we all
          fuckin' agreed this is happening.

                    JI
          No, *you* decided it was happening.
          More people means more problems.

                    OLI
          You got a better idea, jackass?

                    JI
          Oh, fuck you! Don't get so wet
          'cause you finally got a DM in two
          years.

Oli takes a step toward Ji, her fists clenched in anger.

Zola jumps in her way.

                    ZOLA
          Alright, alright, alright! Let's
          just re-vote. Okay? It's fine.

Ji and Oli stand down. Zola takes a deep breath, trying to
restore some sense of order to the situation.

                    ZOLA (CONT'D)
          All who want to stay?

Ji raises his hand while all the others look at him with
annoyance.

                    JI
          Fuck this shit! I'm stayin'! You
          assholes can go play hero without
          me.

Oli pushes past Zola. Despite Ji's bulkier size, she grabs
the older man's vest and pulls him threateningly close to
her. Ji rolls his eyes, unphased by her alpha-leader persona.

                    OLI
          Ain't nobody stayin'. If you're not
          coming with us, you can get the
          fuck out.

The two of them stare each other down for a long moment,
their eyes locked in a battle of wills.

Ji's jaw clenches as the threat sinks in. He glances to the
others who are not making eye contact. He yanks his jacket
from her grasp.

                    JI
          Just remember who called it.

He puts his cigarette back in his mouth and shoulders his
pack. Ji mumbles an insult under his breath as he walks away.

Yuki muffles her laughter. Tim shoots the younger girl a look
to shut up.

Zola hands Oli her pack as she takes the lead toward the exit. Oli is determined to see their mission through to the end - all assholes present.

24   **EXT. OLD TOWN STREET - DAY**

The street is lined with sustainably designed architecture. Curved lines meet natural foliage along the buildings. Deserted vehicles are covered in dust, ash, and debris.

SIX ZOMBIES are spread throughout the block. Their feet shuffle on the pavement as their cataract eyes seek movement in the light.

The crew is spread out along the street. Tim steps forward and opens his palms.

Four beetle-shaped robotic trackers take off into the air. They fly over the zombies ahead.

SWIPT-SWIPT! Two zombies go down from arrows to the head.

Zola reloads his crossbow as the remaining four zombies shuffle along.

                    ZOLA
          Each street is getting thicker, and
          we're getting pushed toward The
          Hive.

                    OLI
          How much farther, Tim?

Oli releases another arrow from her bow. *SWIPT!* Another zombie down a few yards ahead.

Tim's wrist unit projects against his fingers to form a holographic 3D map.

Four red human heat signatures and a gray metallic silhouette mark where the team is on the map. The trackers land and the zombies are identified as green silhouettes further ahead.

                    TIM
          Still gotta get through Old Town
          and up near Doghill. Could be
          another two hours or half a day.

SHRLINK! Ji's billhook blade slices through the neck of another zombie.

                    JI
          I know none of you care, but that
          bad feeling is settling in deep the
          closer we get.

                    YUKI
          Stop being such a pussy. We're at
          least twenty blocks away.

                    JI
          How do you know? It's been weeks
          since we've been up through here.

                    OLI
          Just keep moving. One street at a
          time.

The crew continues their path.

Tim's tracking bugs separate at the next intersection. One
lands on the side of a building. The other is on a window
ledge.

Tim's holographic map lights up the street with FORTY ZOMBIES
on either side of the intersection.

                    TIM
          Oh- shit...

                    OLI
          What?

                    TIM
          ...Um.

                    OLI
          Tim, what?

Oli grabs his wrist and gets a look at his map.

                    OLI (CONT'D)
          Find us another way.

                    JI
          Or...we head back.

                    OLI
          I swear to god, Ji. I'm gonna fuck
          you up.

                    JI
          Just providing options.

25   **EXT. OLD TOWN ALLEYWAY - DAY**

The crew approaches an alleyway nearby. Pressing themselves
against the wall to hide while they wait.

Tim releases three more tracking bugs. They flutter through
the alley cluttered with trash. Calculating the risk and
identifying the threats ahead.

                    JI
          This is a really shitty fucking
          idea.

                    ZOLA
          Maybe we head back?

                    OLI
          No, we get through Cambria, go
          around the horde and get back on
          course to find our survivors.

                    JI
          The Hive already cleaned out
          Cambria. It ain't safe.

                    TIM
          As long as we stay out of Salt Town
          we should be fine.

                    YUKI
          Let's just get this over with,
          please. Tight spaces are bad.

The tracker bugs land further down the long alley. Three
green zombies appear on the holographic map on Tim's palm.

A tracker bug lands on an opening to the alley further down.
A red alert beacon is sent to Tim's pulse unit.

Tim adjusts the map for a wider view. He sees FIFTY ZOMBIES
appear on the street parallel to them.

                    TIM
          Two on the left. One on the right.
          A whole bunch on the other side.

Oli steps to the front and leads with her bow loaded. The
others follow.

SWIPT! A zombie falls to the ground. One zombie further ahead
turns around to investigate. Oli reloads.

Zola shoots his crossbow *SWIPT!* The second zombie falls.

Hunting
Slingshot

The third, unaware of his fallen comrades, shuffles out of range further down.

The crew advances through the narrow space and pauses at an opening that leads to the street littered with zombies.

Tim crosses first, then Yuki, Oli, Ji, and Zola.

They pause against the wall. Tim makes sure they weren't spotted. The horde visible is only a few yards away. Feet shuffling along the pavement, unaware of the living watching from the dark.

While Tim makes his assessment, Yuki watches the remaining threat ahead.

The third zombie left at the end of the alley sniffs the air. His jaw shivers open. He bites at a familiar smell lingering in the breeze.

Yuki watches as he turns in their direction - sniffing and tasting.

She aims her slingshot with a two-inch metal ball. Tapping a button on the projectile, a band of light flickers along the smooth surface.

She fires.

The projectile flies through the air. Four blades emerge from the band of light and begin to spin.

FFFRRRZZZZT! The projectile makes contact with the remaining zombie slicing its head in half.

Yuki clenches her fist in celebration but...

CRASH! CLINK! CLANK!

The zombie falls and lands loudly on a metal trashcan. Its lid rolls down the alleyway and *clatters* to a halt at the crew's feet.

                    YUKI
          Fuck- sorry.

The crew listens as the clatter echoes off the narrow walls.

Silence settles for a long, withheld beat.

The sound of footsteps is heard from the opening they'd just crossed. Tim looks back and spots the horde taking notice.

A grumbling of moans bounce off the narrow space.

                    TIM
          Run- RUN!

Yuki rushes to the zombie she'd just killed. Picking up her
ammo of choice. Oli snatches her arm and launches her
forward.

                    OLI
          Are you fucking kidding me?

                    ZOLA
          Move! Move!

                    JI
          I told you--

They sprint down the alleyway. The ZOMBIE HORDE OF 50 chases
after them. For every zombie that stumbles, another climbs
over it.

A wave of undead bodies grows larger. Their mass as one
struggling to morph into a line gives our heroes a chance.

The crew break out onto...

26   **EXT. CAMBRIA STREET #1 - CONTINUOUS**

Oli and Yuki bolt out on an open street. The buildings here
are taller, sleeker, more curved, and shiny.

The two-way road is wide. Deserted vehicles clutter the path.

Tim is lagging behind the rest of the crew. He taps his wrist
unit and hits "REPOSITION."

The trackers take flight from their positions on lamp posts
and buildings nearby.

Flying over the horde and ahead of the running crew, the
distance between the two is shortening.

The first tracker lands on the side of a building up ahead.

A HIVE BEE hovers past and approaches the road where the crew
is running for their lives.

The mechanical threat is powered by a propulsion system. Its
mechanical legs dangle like a metal bee.

On its side is a nameplate that reads, "Sanctuary Recovery
Droid."

Yuki slides to a halt first. She points ahead.

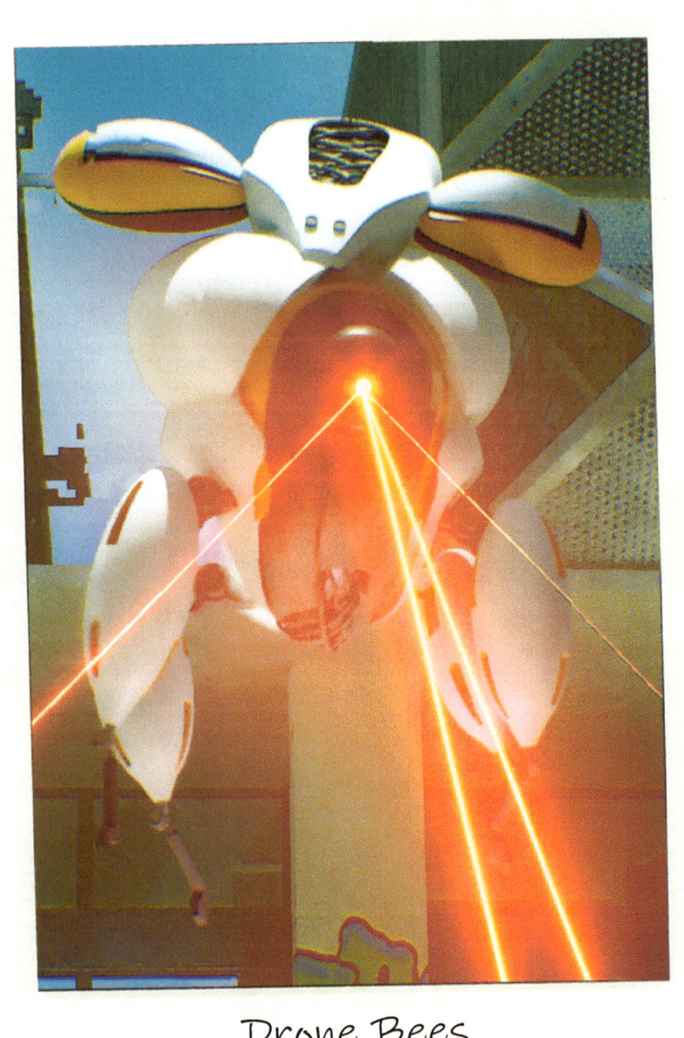

Drone Bees

OH
FUCK!

                    YUKI
          BEES!

Yuki's hair and clothes are hit by a wall of wind.

She stands in shock as the large floating Hive Bee turns the
corner.

                    OLI
          Fuck!

Oli grabs Yuki out of the windy downwash and pulls her out of
the way.

The Hive Bee scans the street. The four human crew members
are identified with red thermal silhouettes hiding around the
corner.

The zombie threat is quickly locked on by their green thermal
readings.

The Hive Bee activates its weapons system.

Tim is ducking down behind a deserted bus, unaware of the
threat.

He is focused on his holographic map, trying to find a path
on the streets ahead.

THE ZOMBIE HORDE IS GETTING CLOSER!

Yuki jumps away from the street corner when she notices Tim's
position.

                    YUKI
          TIM! GET OUT OF THERE!

Ji yanks up Yuki by the waist and returns to cover.

Tim looks up just in time to see the Hive Bee unleashing a
shower of hot white lasers.

The light bullets take down a Zombie as it leaps over a car
toward Tim.

Tim darts around the bus, narrowly avoiding the shots.

The zombie horde falls to the ground, decimated by the
continuous line of light bullets.

The Hive Bee passes Tim. He gets up and joins the others who
have made it to...

27   **EXT. CAMBRIA INTERSECTION - CONTINUOUS**

Oli, Ji, Zola, Yuki, and Tim huddle against a wall, panting
for breath.

                    JI
          I told you! I fucking told--

                    OLI
          We can't go back now. We ditch the
          Bee and keep going.

                    TIM
          Who'd it lock onto?

They each shrug and shake their heads, unsure.

                    OLI
          Let's not wait and find out. We
          take separate routes to throw it
          off. Once we're out of the
          territory, it won't follow.

Oli extends her hand and her wrist unit projects a similar
map to Tim's. She places a marker on a building that lights
up and reads, "Culinary Center."

                    OLI (CONT'D)
          We'll hunker down at the Culinary
          Center.

                    ZOLA
          But that's in Salt Town. You just
          said--

                    TIM
          It's outside of their pollinating
          zone - we should be fine.

Ji shakes his head and laughs at the absurdity of their
situation. Oli and Zola take off down their own paths.

                    YUKI
          I'm sorry. It's my fault.

                    TIM
          Hey! You gotta focus. I'm with you
          all the way, okay?

Yuki nods.

                    YUKI
               (to Ji)
          Maybe you were right.

                    JI
          I usually am.

Tim grabs Yuki's arm and leads her away.

Ji peeks around the corner to see the Hive Bee mowing down
the zombies trying to escape the alley.

28   **EXT. CAMBRIA STREET #2 - CONTINUOUS**

Zola jogs down the side of a one-way street, crossbow at the
ready.

He stops to catch his breath on the stoop of an abandoned
coffee shop.

Checking his wrist unit he pulls up a map similar to Tim's.
All the heat readings are behind him.

                    ZOLA
          Take me to the culinary center.
          Fastest route.

A path appears on the 3D map, curving through the streets to
the destination.

Zola takes a few more deep breaths before stepping off the
stoop.

He is met by the humming of a Hive Bee waiting for him.

Zola's eyes widen as he backs away from the threat.

As he turns, a tranquilizer dart shoots out from the Hive Bee
and lands in Zola's back. He gasps for air as his legs lock
up.

Before he can fall, the Hive Bee's four large metal legs open
up and engulf him.

29   **EXT. CAMBRIA ALLEYWAY - CONTINUOUS**

Oli runs through an alley, loading her bow as she goes.

She approaches the outlet, but a HIVE BEE BLOCKS HER EXIT!

She retreats in the opposite direction.

The Hive Bee is too large for the alley. It releases TWO
SURVEILLANCE DRONES that follow her. They both fire darts.

Surveillance Drone 2 makes contact with Oli's neck.

She attempts to reach behind her, but her legs lock up, her eyes close, and she falls forward.

30   **EXT. CAMBRIA STREET #3 - DAY**

Yuki and Tim are sprinting down a deserted street. They hop over a parked car.

Tim spots an abandoned warehouse nearby.

                    TIM
          This way!

They turn the corner and make their way to...

31   **EXT. WAREHOUSE BUILDING - CONTINUOUS**

Tim helps Yuki climb up near a window in the side of the warehouse. Just as Yuki opens the window, Tim hears a BUZZING from around the corner.

He pushes Yuki forcefully into the building.

                    YUKI
          Hey! Dont push! Dont push!

KERTHUNK! Yuki hits the floor.

                    TIM
          Stay there. I'll be back.

Tim runs into the middle of the street, waving his arms.

                    TIM (CONT'D)
          Hey! Over here! Come and get me!

The Hive Bee turns toward his voice. Its thermal reading not acknowleding his gray metallic signature.

On his pulse unit Tim turns on his "Thermal Mode." The Hive Bee picks up on the new heat signature.

A chase begins.

32   **INT. WAREHOUSE BUILDING - DAY**

Yuki recovers from her fall into a pile of boxes. Once she is able to get her footing, she surveys the warehouse.

The open space is filled with toppled shelves and stacked pallets.

Bionic
Leg &
Jaw

Bionic
Arms

Bionic
Ears

Clink-Clank! A metal noise echoes in the dark.

Yuki ducks behind a stack of boxes, trying to stay out of sight. She spots something moving in the darkness.

A human figure steps into the light and moves closer. Yuki strains her eyes to focus.

ZOMBORG 1, a zombie with bionic arms and legs, steps into the light. He sniffs the air.

ARCKH-ARCKH-ARCKH! The fleshy mutated jaw CHOMPs the air between sniffs.

Yuki's eyes widen as she tries to get up, but her foot slips on loose dirt.

Zomborg 1 locks into her sound. It slowly crouches down to all fours and sniffs the air again. Yuki's face fills with terror.

THE CREATURE LEAPS TOWARD HER. YUKI GETS HER FOOTING AND RUNS!!

ZOMBORG 1 IS GAINING ON HER. IT'S MOUTH FOAMING!

BLAM! Yuki escapes through the exit onto...

33   **EXT. WAREHOUSE BUILDING - CONTINUOUS**

Yuki *SLAMS* the door behind her. Zomborg 1 rams against it.

BANG-BANG-BANG! The metal door bows and the hinges crack.

Yuki backs away trying to catch her breath.

WOOOOORRRRSSSSHHH!!! A gust of air from a Hive Bee's propulsion system blows her hair forward. She turns just in time to see a metal dart hit her in the neck.

The metal door flies off the hinges as the Zomborg emerges.

The Hive Bee wraps its metal arms around Yuki and accelerates upward.

ZOMBORG 1 JUMPS UP TO BITE YUKI'S LEGS - BUT MISSES BY MEERE INCHES!

34   **EXT. CAMBRIA STREET #4 - CONTINUOUS**

Tim runs back toward the warehouse. He watches in terror as Yuki's body dangles in the Hive Bee's legs.

The Bee's metal stomach opens up and swallows the girl whole.

Tim tries not to panic as the Bee takes off. He dips into an alley and uses parkour to scale the wall.

35   **EXT. CAMBRIA ROOFTOPS - CONTINUOUS**

Tim makes his way to the roof. He spots three Hive Bees flying off in the distance.

He leaps from roof to roof, trying to keep pace. He gets to a ledge with a gap that's too wide.

He grabs his futuristic baton from his hip and presses a button. A shiney metal javelin extends.

Tim backs up and runs towards the edge. He slams the tip of his javelin into the ground and uses it to pole vault his body through the air.

Ji can be seen on the street below, looking up in disbelief.

                    JI
          ...The fuck?

Tim crashes through the window of...

36   **INT. ABANDONED OFFICE BUILDING - CONTINUOUS**

Glass shatters as Tim falls to the ground, sliding across the office floor.

Sitting up, he groans.

ZOMBORG 2, an elderly female with a bionic arm, sniffs the air to Tim's left. Her jaw chomps down at nothing. ***ARKCH!***

Tim stands up, quickly scanning the area for his javelin.

ZOMBORG 3, a male with metal ears and gouged-out eyes, is creeping closer to Tim. Sniffing and chomping. ***ARKCH-ARKCH!***

Tim backs away, edging closer to the open window ledge. He spots his javelin between the two zomborgs.

Zomborg 2 lunges towards Tim. He dodges the attack and picks up a file sorter. Throwing it at the threat.

Zomborg 3 hones in on the sound and approaches with precision.

Tim gets blocked in and throws whatever he can at the
approaching modified zombies.

                    TIM
          Janice, did you get the memo about
          not biting in the office?

Zomborg 2 goes limp as a javelin punctures through her
temple. *VVRRKKKT!*

Tim looks over to see Ji smiling.

                    JI
          Nice jump, idiot.

Blind Zomborg 3 turns toward Ji's voice, chomping at the air.
ARKCH-ARKCH!

Ji splits the creature's head in half with a single blow of
his billhook. **THWACK!**

Blood splatters mostly on Ji and a little on Tim's shirt.

                    TIM
          Jesus, Ji! Really?

                    JI
          What? I saved you?

                    TIM
          Ugh! C'mon! The bees got Yuki.

                    JI
          Shit.

Tim claims his javelin from the skull of Zomborg 2 and moves
through the door.

Ji follows after him.

37   **EXT. ROOF OF ABANDONED OFFICE BUILDING - CONTINUOUS**

KRBLAM! Tim charges out of the roof access door, looking up
at the sky.

His javelin at the ready, he rushes to the edge of the
building.

Ji exits the access door catching his breath.

VWWIP! A dart lands in Ji's neck. He goes limp.

VRRRRRROOOSSSSHHHH! A Hive Bee scoops Ji up into its metal
legs.

The Bee's stomach opens up with a rush of cold air. Ji's body
is engulfed into it's belly.

CLINK! Tim throws his javelin at the Hive Bee, but it bounces
off as the machine gains altitude.

>   TIM
>   No! No! No! What is happening? What
>   is *happening*!?

Tim follows the Hive Bee to the other side of the roof.

He spots all four Hive Bees heading toward a LARGE GRAY WALL
towering over small buildings in the distance.

SUPER: THE HIVE

Tim is alone and unable to follow.

<u>END ACT 3</u>

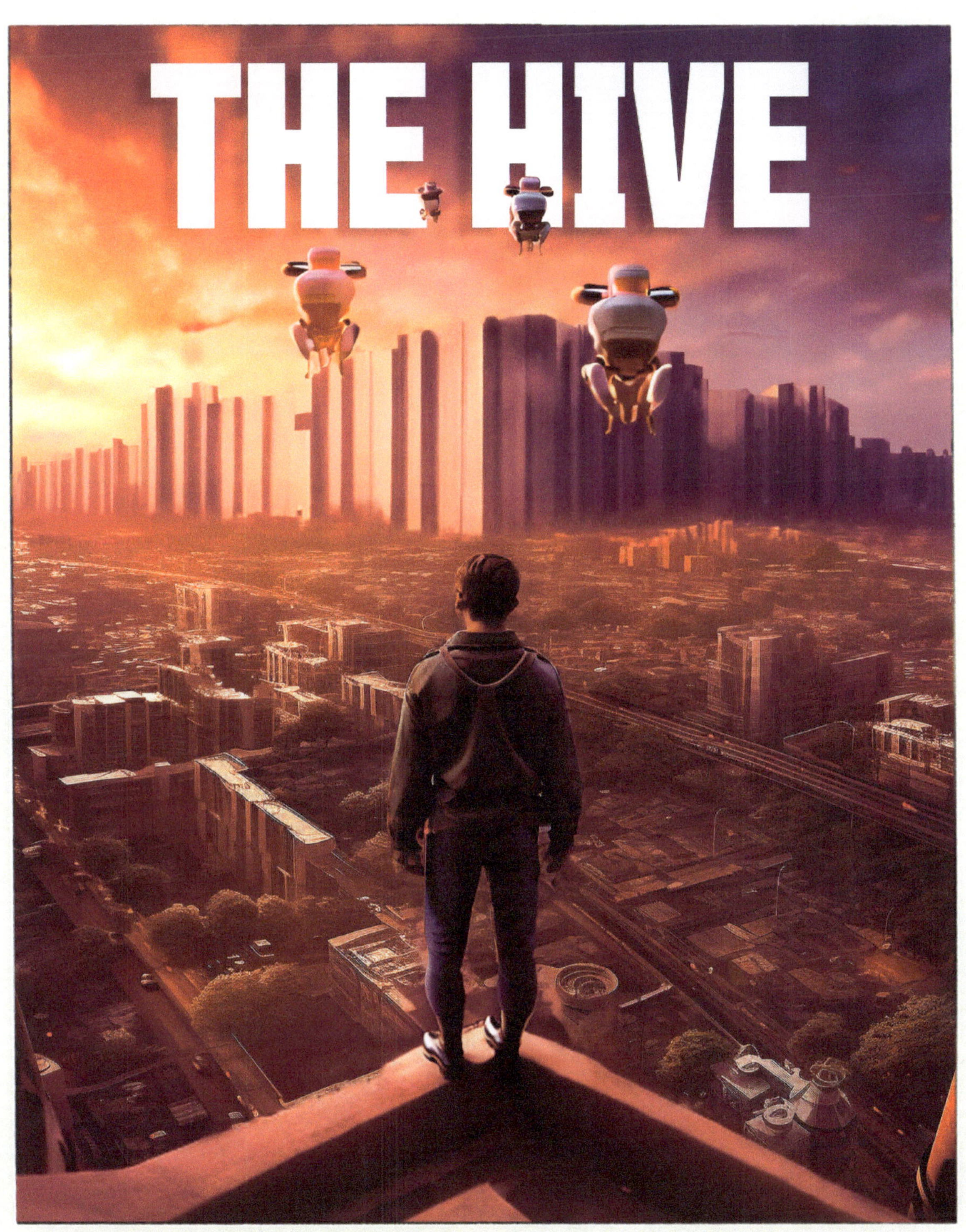

THE HIVE

ACT 4

38   **INT. SANCTUARY WELCOME ROOMS - MORNING**

Yuki gasps as she sits up, panting, and disoriented. The
events of her capture catch up to her in that waking moment.

She glances around, realizing she is the first to wake in a
large circular room. Her other teammates are unconscious, but
their presence calms her.

She inspects her new wardrobe. The gray athleisure wear is
soft and comfortable. A digital armband is strapped to her
left arm. The flexible screen of the band emits a white
number 1 on a red background.

Without warning, Oli stands up from her cot, ready for a
fight. The older woman looks around at the others and makes
eye contact with Yuki.

                    OLI
          You okay, kid?

                    YUKI
          Yeah...

Zola's hands flail violently around as he wakes, trying to
defend himself from invisible assailants. His breathing is
frantic before he notices the two females nearby.

                    ZOLA
          Where are we?

                    OLI
          ... don't know.

Ji begins to snore from his cot, unaware of his comrades'
rude awakenings.

BRRRMMMMM... The holograph orb in the center of the room hums
and begins to glow. The surrounding lights of the space dim
to give a sense of importance to the presentation starting
up.

Oli moves to stand next to Yuki as a mother would her young.
Zola attempts to shake Ji awake, but he shrugs his shoulders
to be left alone.

Zola tilts the cot to its side, and the large man hits the
floor hard. **BLAM!**

                    JI
          I'm up!

Grey
Athleisure
Wardrobe

Sactuary
Arm
Bands

Welcome
Room

The crew surrounds the hologram orb as it begins to play.

39   **EXT. THE SANCTUARY PROPAGANDA HOLOGRAM - DAY**

A futuristic town square fades into view. The buildings are curved and organic in shape. The street is empty, clean, and well-maintained. Storefronts display their services and workmanship in large windows. There's a shine to the little town that seems manufactured and perfect.

AMALA VON BRANDT, the Nuvitta Corporation CEO, 60's, stands in the middle of the road.

                    AMALA
          Hello. My name is Amala Von Brandt
          and on behalf of the Nuvitta
          Corporation, I'd like to welcome
          you to The Sanctuary District.

SUPER: "WELCOME TO SANCTUARY"

The hologram transitions to the scene of a meteor falling over the Nuvitta skyline at sunset.

Security footage shows the meteor crashing into a convenience store. The large rock expels a cloud of spores into the air.

A SURVIVOR, fatally injured from the crash, is laying on the ground. They begin coughing and thrashing. A SECOND SURVIVOR approaches to help, only to be viscously attacked by the first.

                    AMALA VO
          The last two years have been...
          terrible. With the rise in the
          fungal infection, X80, our once
          immaculate city of Nuvitta has
          fallen to barbaric deaths and
          extreme violence.

The hologram transitions to security footage on an exterior street. A woman is fighting off a zombie in the park.

A second transition reveals a group of survivors taking to the streets with weapons. They are fighting back against the violent infected only to be turned themselves.

                    AMALA VO (CONT'D)
          We know you've done what was
          necessary to survive. And we
          commend our citizens on your
          ability to adapt in the face of
          adversity.

"THE HIVE"

AKA:
The Sanctuary
District

The hologram morphs to a scene of Amala sitting on a bench
next to a park.

                    AMALA
          But now... now is the time to get
          back to how things were. To rebuild
          and reconnect with our once
          flourishing community.

TWO TEENS run past Amala's bench kicking a soccer ball.

                    AMALA (CONT'D)
          To let kids be kids. And to join
          together with other survivors to
          rebuild what was once our home.

The hologram dissolves to show a bird's-eye view of
Sanctuary. The residential homes are similar in design and
built close together.

                    AMALA VO
          In Sanctuary, we've returned to our
          system of guaranteed state-of-the-
          art housing.

Without transition, the hologram flies into one of the
streets where TWO GUARDS are casually on patrol.

                    AMALA VO (CONT'D)
          We've implemented a security
          program of neighbors and friends.

THREE TEENS are playing a futuristic version of soccer in one
of the yards.

A PREGNANT MOTHER calls out the door to one of the teenagers
to come in. The YOUNG TEEN rushes in to find his FATHER and
BROTHER preparing to sit down for a meal.

                    AMALA VO (CONT'D)
          Making it a safe place to raise
          children and start thinking about
          the future.

The hologram fades into pixels and respawns a delivery truck
pulling up to a grocery store.

The STORE MANAGER scans the delivery of fresh fruits.

Shoppers pick out fresh fruits and vegetables.

                    AMALA VO (CONT'D)
          The Nuvitta Corporation has been
          able to bring back meaningful work,
          guaranteed access to water, and
          healthy foods. All are made
          available to the community, by the
          community.

The hologram morphs to A TEEN GIRL in an education pod. She
is engaging in a hologram lesson that portrays whales
swimming around her with names and stats tracked to each
creature.

                    AMALA VO (CONT'D)
          Most importantly, we have built a
          state-of-the-art education facility
          to continue our children's growth.
          Without our children, there is no
          future. So guaranteeing they have
          the best is a top priority for
          everyone here in Nuvitta.

The hologram dissolves back to Amala standing in the town
square, surrounded by other residents.

                    AMALA
          The road ahead is a long one, but
          we have a wonderful foundation for
          recovery. We're all in this
          together. And we are all very
          excited to have you.

The residents wave and smile.

SUPER "WELCOME HOME!"

40   **INT. SANCTUARY WELCOME ROOMS – CONTINUOUS**

The holographic orb projects a spinning "Welcome Home" in 3D
text.

The crew of four glances at one another with expressions of
confusion.

                    JI
          So we're... we're dead.

                    OLI
          Captives at most.

                    ZOLA
          Are we in wait-and-see mode or--

                        YUKI
                --Where's Tim?

It's at that moment the crew realizes they're missing one.

41   **EXT. ALLEY NEAR THE HIVE - DAY**

The wall, known to the crew as "The Hive," towers over the
city at twenty-five stories tall. Large vents produce a cloud
of ominous steam that billows into the air.

A wired fence surrounds a desolate parking lot that looks
like a giant moat of blacktop around the structure.

Tim, is across the street from the wired fence. He is hiding
behind a vehicle as he evaluates the structure before him.

A large ventilation grate a few yards from the main entrance
is spotted. It's not producing any steam or smoke.

VRRSSSHHHHH... A HIVE BEE, on patrol, turns the corner a few
blocks down. Tim backs cautiously into a narrow alley and
ducks behind a large dumpster to stay out of view.

The Hive Bee uses its scanning system on vehicles and
storefront windows. It gets closer to Tim's hiding spot.

Frantic he taps at his wrist unit. Flipping through menues to
turn off his "Thermal Mode."

A red line scans the dumpster as Tim presses his body against
the wall and attempts to remain as still as possible.

When the Hive Bee detects nothing, it continues down the
street. Turning to the next block - out of sight.

Tim watches it go. Then turns his attention back to the
fortress he knows he'll have to infiltrate.

42   **INT. ALMA VON BRANDT'S OFFICE - DAY**

The office of Alma Von Brandt is well-decorated with modern
art, large windows, and curved furniture.

The CEO is dressed in a white lab coat in front of a large
hologram table at the center of the room. She is examining
what looks to be digitized 3D brain scans fused with wires
and metals.

ADAM PORTER, 60's, is with Amala keeping notes on a tablet.
Neither of them wears an armband.

                    AMALA
          Life expectancy was how long?

                    ADAM
          76 hours.

SHHHWWWSHHH - the mechanic circular doors open. Amala
casually turns off the hologram.

MOIRA CUNNINGHAM, 30's, enters dressed in a gray fitted shirt
and pants. A digital armband emits a faint PURPLE LIGHT and a
white number 6. She places a stack of folders on the desk.

                    MOIRA
          I have the reports. The girl is
          definitely going to be of interest.

The four folders have names and an old photograph of each
crew member. Amala takes up Yuki's folder. Adam takes up
Oli's.

                    MOIRA (CONT'D)
          They've watched the introductory
          sequence. Should I continue them
          through Step One?

Amala points at something in the folder and Adam makes an
impressed face.

                    AMALA
          Yes, dear. Let's make them feel as
          comfortable as possible. They may
          be a little more apprehensive than
          the others considering how long
          they've been out in the wild.

Moira nods and leaves.

                    ADAM
          Thirteen's young.

                    AMALA
          Thirteen's a perfectly good age.

43   **INT. SANCTUARY WELCOME ROOMS - SUNSET**

The crew stand around Yuki's Cot, huddled together for
privacy and comfort.

                    JI
          What we thinkin'?

                    ZOLA
          It's definitely high-quality
          propaganda.

                    YUKI
          I don't like it.

                    OLI
          Let's say this is real. Maybe we
          were wrong about what's been going
          on here.

                    YUKI
          Why didn't they blast the info over
          a loudspeaker or something?

                    ZOLA
          Or fix the network with these
          resources.

                    JI
          Misunderstandings happen in a war
          zone--

The door of the room slides open and the crew stands up.

                    OLI
               (lowered voice)
          Whatever happens, we stick
          together...

MOIRA enters with a digital tablet in hand.

                    JI
          Hey! Ain't seen no chick in a
          while.

Oli and Yuki smack him in both arms. He flinches.

                    MOIRA
          Hello, welcome to The Sanctuary
          District. I'm Moira, and I'm here
          to help you with any questions --

                    OLI
          --Yeah, where are we?

                    MOIRA
          Didn't you watch the--

                    ZOLA
          -- It didn't explain where or why
          exactly.

                    MOIRA
          Oh, well, you were rescued from the
          extract zone and--

                    YUKI
          --More like kidnapped.

                    MOIRA
          I know this might all seem very
          different than what you're used to.
          But, I'd love to show you around.

                    JI
          Let's do it.

Oli sticks her hand out to stop Ji from following.

                    OLI
          Why should we follow you?

                    MOIRA
          Again, I'm Moira. I'm here to get
          you settled in. So, if you'll
          follow me, we'll get started on the
          first phase of your integration.

Without waiting, Moira walks down the hallway, speaking.

44   **INT. SANCTUARY WELCOME CENTER HALLWAY - CONTINUOUS**

The marble floors of the hallway and the retro green
wallpaper are lit with modern sconces. Moira is talking as
the crew pick up pace to join her.

                    MOIRA (CONT)
          The Sanctuary District is the
          Nuvitta Corporation's solution to
          the X80 pandemic. Over the last two
          years we've been able to establish
          an impenetrable barrier with our
          state-of-the-art wall. We've been
          sending recovery drones to collect
          survivors over the last 23 months
          and--

                    OLI
          -- Why didn't you let people know?

                    MOIRA
          We did. We brought them here.

                    ZOLA
          What about the people you left
          behind?

                    MOIRA
          The Nuvitta Network went down some
          hours after the outbreak began. It
          was impossible to contact outside
          of the Sanctuary District.

                    JI
          Wait so ... this is The Hive? So
          you're a... you know.

                    MOIRA
          ...A what?

                    YUKI
          A zomborg. He's asking if you're a
          zomborg.

                    MOIRA
          I'm sorry?

                    YUKI
          A modified upgrader who's been
          bitten.

                    MOIRA
          Oh! No! Most of us started out just
          like you. We were all picked up by
          the Nuvitta security drones and
          brought to safety.

They pass by a series of large windows overlooking the
Sanctuary grounds. One by one, the crew members slow down.
Taking in their new civilized surroundings.

The neighborhood is free of zombies. Electric vehicles move
down one-way streets. People buzz about their everyday tasks.
No one is dressed in survival gear or equipped with weapons.

                    OLI
          Why not put the effort into
          cleaning up the city?

                    MOIRA
          Well, the Nuvitta Corporation
          determined that it would be easier
          to recover a smaller district
          first. But now that the Network
          was rebooted, we can start turning
          our efforts outward.

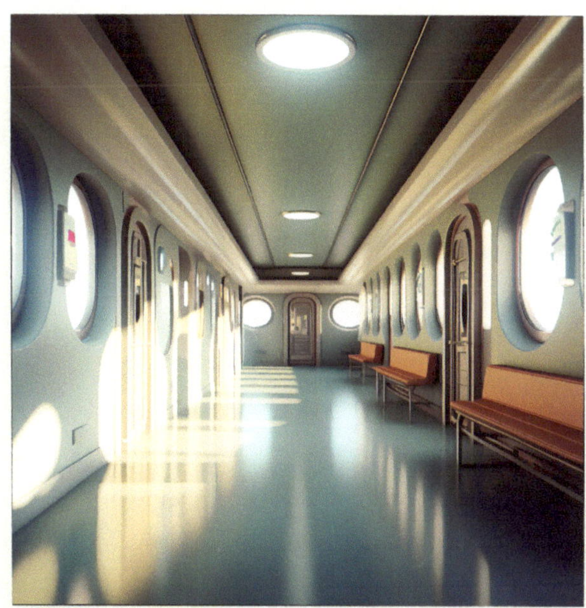

                    JI
              (to Yuki)
          Told you we'd attract something.

                    MOIRA
          Wait, you fixed it?

                    OLI
          Yeah... we were looking for
          survivors.

                    MOIRA
          That's wonderful. We're all hoping
          that we'll be able to use the
          Network to track down others who're
          still out there.

                    YUKI
          What about our friend Tim? Where's
          he?

Moira glances at her tablet for a moment.

                    MOIRA
          Hmm... I only have records of four.

                    YUKI
          We're definitely five.

                    MOIRA
          I'll have them run another search
          for your fifth.

                    YUKI
          Search? He's still out there?

                    MOIRA
          What's his name?

                    ZOLA
          Tim Russo.

                    JI
          He's probably fine, kid. Tim's
          resourceful.

                    YUKI
          We have to get him.

Moira pauses a moment as she looks at her screen. Oli is the
only one who notices the other woman's masked confusion.

They watch as Moira taps at a few buttons and then looks up
with a smile.

                    MOIRA
          I have a team out now. How about we
          get you to your new home while we
          wait?

                    ZOLA
          We're housed together, right?

                    MOIRA
          Of course. Follow me.

Moira moves onward. The crew exchange glances before
following.

                    YUKI
               (To Oli)
          What if they don't find him?

                    OLI
          Then we'll do it ourselves.
          Promise.

45   **EXT. STREET SURROUNDING HIVE - SUNSET**

Tim crouches behind a parked vehicle near the fenced parking
lot. He watches as TWO SURVEILLANCE DRONES glide past.

When it's clear, he moves to another car.

WREEEE-WRREEE-WREEE! The car alarm goes off!

TIM JUMPS AND RUNS TO HIDE AROUND THE CORNER OF THE NEAREST
BUILDING!

The drones turn around to investigate the sound.

WREEEE-WRREEE-WREEE!

The alarm attracts a Hive Bee who joins the two drones. They
begin scanning the road nearby.

WREEEE-WRREEE-WREEE!

Tim takes another glance at the ventilation grate.

Surveillance Drone 2 harpoons a cord into the vehicle and
sends an electrical shock to disable it.

Silence.

A ***RUMBLING SOUND*** draws Tim's attention behind him.

A HORDE of 150 ZOMBIES rush down the road, attracted by the car alarm.

They look like a wave of bodies toppeling over abandoned cars, and funneling down the street.

TIM RUNS! THE HOARD JOINS HIM A FEW FEET BEHIND!

HE IS LEADING THE HORDE!!!

46   **EXT. THE HIVE ENTRANCE - CONTINUOUS**

Tim scales the fence quickly and sprints toward the wall.

Seconds later, the horde burst through the metal fence. They move like a mass of bodies toward the towering wall.

The Hive Bee and its surveillance drones open fire on the wave of zombies from behind. A flury of white hot bullets rain down from the sky.

Tim slides to a halt as the wall's defenses are activated. Zombies rush past him. He's now mixed in with the approaching mass of undead.

A MILITARIZED HIVE BEE is released from the 10th-story drone bay, shooting down the zombies in front of our gangly hero.

TIM TRIES TO RUN IN THE OTHER DIRECTION BUT REALIZES HE IS CAUGHT IN THE CROSSFIRE!

Light bullets violently zip down from both sides, hitting his chest, back, legs, and arms.

He falls to the ground. Zombies climb over him to get through. As they are annihilated by the bullets, bodies pile on top of Tim Russo.

<u>END ACT 4</u>

ACT 5

47 **EXT. SANCTUARY INTAKE TUNNEL - MAGIC HOUR**

An autonomous hovercraft buzzes down a solar roadway tunnel.
Lights flickering against the smooth surface. In the vehicle
our four crew members and Moira are seated facing one
another.

                    ZOLA
          How many survivors are here?

                    MOIRA
          Our current population is twenty-
          seven-thousand, one hundred and
          seventy-four. We anticipate natural
          growth over the next year.

                    OLI
          How many more survivors do you
          think are even out there?

                    MOIRA
          Oh, we're not sure. You're the
          biggest group we've picked up in
          months. But our birthing program
          has increased since spring.

                    YUKI
          Babies?

                    MOIRA
          Yes. We have about twenty-four
          pregnant women within Sanctuary.
          All are being protected and taken
          care of.

                    ZOLA
          That's...incredible.

The hovercraft emerges from the tunnel. A series of four-
story shops and apartments rush past.

Everything is clean, new, and zombie-free. The crew leans
into the window to get a better look as the last bit of
sunset disappears.

Streetlights begin to flicker on. Each person has an armband
of different colors and numbers.

                    ZOLA (CONT'D)
          What are the bands for?

                    MOIRA
          You'll find out at your educational
          orientation in a day or two. It'll
          explain everything.

                    YUKI
          Why can't you explain it now?

                    MOIRA
          That's not how this works.

                    OLI
          Maybe it should be.

                    MOIRA
          I promise the armbands will be
          explained, but right now what's
          important is getting you into your
          new housing. Making you feel safe.

                    YUKI
          Yeah, right.

                    JI
          Hey! They gotta bar.

Ji points out the window excitedly.

                    MOIRA
          Yes...it's limited in their
          selection, but it's a good place to
          meet people.

48   **EXT. RESIDENTIAL DISTRICT - DUSK**

BWONG! A community chime echoes over the residential district
signaling the end of day.

The vehicle transporting the crew moves down a one-way
residential street.

The buildings are quaint 3D-printed homes. Solar-powered
street lights glow as pedestrians make their way home.

49   **INT. CREW'S SANCTUARY HOME - DUSK**

Moira enters a curved doorway, followed by the crew. The
automatic lights turn on and reveal a smooth white interior
of an open floorplan. The furniture is modern with pops of
color.

                    MOIRA
          Welcome to your new home. You'll
          find two bedrooms and a fully
          stocked kitchen.

Ji goes directly to the fridge. It's stuffed with fruits,
veggies, and a selection of beverages. He locates a beer and
chugs it.

Zola examines the bedroom to the left while Oli checks out
the bedroom on the right.

Yuki remains in the living room with Moira.

                    YUKI
          What's the catch?

                    MOIRA
          What do you mean?

                    YUKI
          Why are you housing us?

                    MOIRA
          You were probably too young to
          remember, but every basic need is
          provided by The Nuvitta
          Corporation. Food, water, shelter.

                    YUKI
          What do we have to do for you?

                    MOIRA
          It's not for me. It's for the
          community. We're all in this
          together, right?

                    OLI
          I assume we're given jobs in
          exchange? Like before?

                    MOIRA
          Yes, exactly. We've done a citizen
          scan and have assigned jobs based
          on your previous posts.

She reaches into her pocket and hands out four metal cards.

                    MOIRA (CONT'D)
          If you would prefer a fresh start
          in a different position, do let us
          know. It shouldn't be a problem.

Yuki reads her card with silver engraving, *"Nuvitta Sanctuary Educational Facility - 8am - Mon-Thurs."*

> YUKI
> School? Seriously?

> MOIRA
> Education is one of the largest
> pillars in Nuvitta. It'll be good
> for you.

Yuki rolls her eyes.

50   **INT. SANCUTARY OBSERVATION DECK - NIGHT**

A surveillance feed shows Moira leaving the crew of four in their new home.

The screen is on a wall that includes hundreds of other video feeds. Sactuary homes, streets, and the surrounding city of the protective wall are being watched.

51   **INT. SECURITY PATROL OFFICE - DAY**

Oli and JI are escorted by OFFICER MILLIGAN, a 50-something woman wearing a dark red uniform. Her armband emits a white light with a blue number 7 on it.

The hallway is white marble, immaculately clean, with a line down the middle to direct traffic.

Ji and Oli notice other security patrol officers staring as they pass.

> MILLIGAN
> According to your files, this ain't
> your first post?

> OLI
> Thirteen years on droid patrol.

> JI
> I was executive security for four
> years.

> MILLIGAN
> Well, here in Sanctuary we ain't
> got droids or executives, so you'll
> both be patrol officers.

> OLI
> Why is that? No droids?

Milligan stops at the end of the hall in front of a
futuristic automat of windows. She taps a few numbers on the
screen, and the window emits light.

>   MILLIGAN
>   Most droids are fugus powered.
>   Better safe than sorry, right?

>   OLI
>   But... X80 is airborne, we're all
>   infected.

Milligan retrieves two uniform bags from the window and hands
them to Oli and Ji.

>   MILLIGAN
>   You're not gonna be one of those,
>   are you?

>   OLI
>   What?

>   MILLIGAN
>   Someone who thinks they know better
>   than us?

>   OLI
>   I was just-- No... sorry.

>   MILLIGAN
>   Great.
>   (to Ji)
>   What about you?

>   JI
>   I don't know much about anything,
>   so carry on.

She hands each of them an ELECTRO BATON.

>   MILLIGAN
>   Your electro batons have to be
>   checked in and out at every shift.
>   Don't take it home with you. Don't
>   forget to charge it either.

Oli takes the baton and looks awkwardly at Ji, who makes a
face.

Milligan continues down the hall.

>   MILLIGAN (CONT'D)
>   Suit up, your first assignment is
>   perimeter cleanup.

EXT. WALL OUTER PERIMETER - DAY

The smooth cement wall towers high, casting a long shadow
over its surroundings. The grinding sound of the large gate
echoes across the vast parking lot.

Two large military vehicles exit and separate on either side
of the gate.

Gatling guns, self-manned, shoot down the zombies rushing
toward the perimeter.

Two military drones assist in shutting down the undead
advance. The last shot echoes through the empty streets
beyond, and silence falls for a long beat.

The doors of the military vehicles unlock and open. Six
patrol officers exit from the back. Each is wearing a red
uniform.

Oli and Ji begin dragging zombie bodies off the black top.

>   JI
>   They got bots for shootin' em, but
>   no bots for cleanin' up?

>   OLI
>   For such a high-end facility it's
>   definitely lacking, isn't it?

>   JI
>   Just more proof, no one knows what
>   the fuck they're doing.

Oli bends down to move a zombie revealing Tim's lifeless body
underneath.

>   OLI
>   Holy shit. Ji- JI!

She drops to her knees and shakes Tim slightly. Ji rushes
over and shakes him harder.

Tim's entire chest and back are riddled with holes, and one
of his eyes is missing. A blue and white substance drips from
his wounds.

His good eye stares up at the sky, lifeless.

>   FADE TO BLACK

TO BE CONTINUED...

HEY! YOU JUST READ A PILOT! THAT, OR YOU'RE A LAZY BASTARD WHO JUST THUMBED YOUR WAY TO THIS SECTION. EITHER WAY, THE NEXT BIT IS FOR THOSE WHO SIMPLY CAN'T WAIT TO DEVOUR MORE OF THIS ZOMBORG BIRTHDAY CAKE. THE PITCH BOOK IS A LIL' MORE ABOUT THE WORLD, THE CHARACTERS, AND THE EPISODES TO COME.
NOW GO TAKE A LEAK, HIT THE BONG, AND COME BACK TO DEVOUR MORE OF SURVIVORS DON'T DIE.
Civilians
Zola
Ji
Oli
Tim
Yuki
Amala

SURVIVORS
DON'T DIE
Pitch Book
Episode #1

In a world besieged by cybernetic zombies, a group of survivors finds false sanctuary within a corporate utopia, only to uncover that the true terror may not be the zomborgs prowling outside, but the corporate machinations within.

INTRO

SURVIVORS DON'T DIE zooms us into 2123, where the world's playing a high-stakes game of survival against cyborg zombies. Enter the Sanctuary District, humanity's last "safe spot," courtesy of the benevolent Nuvitta Corporation.

Spoiler alert: their definition of safety might include some fine print.

Leading our tour through this future dystopia is a squad that's more mismatched than socks in a laundry basket. We've got Oli Callahan, the brains. Yuki and Tim Russo, the tech whizzes who probably reboot zombies for fun. Dr. Zola Bule, the skeptical mediator. And Ji Hardy, who's all muscle and maybe more heart than he'd admit. Together, they're about to learn that the zombies clawing at the gates might be the least of their worries.

Dive deeper with them into Sanctuary's glossy exterior. The Program, led by the mysterious CEO Amala Von Brandt, might just be the cure for humanity. Here, survivors are holding on to a life of comfort, as Nuvitta's shadowy agenda threatens the core of what it means to be human.

SURVIVORS DON'T DIE is more than just a survival tale with a side of corporate espionage. It's a poke at identity, humanity, and the price of a utopia sponsored by the folks who probably caused the mess in the first place.

Set against a backdrop of techno-terrors and a company that's too shady for comfort, this series is a wild ride. What happens when the future we dreamed of becomes the nightmare we didn't see coming? Will our unlikely heroes navigate this mess, or will they find themselves wishing for the simpler times of just dodging regular old zombies?

WE ARE ALL IN THIS TOGETHER

In 2020, at the brink of the Covid-19 pandemic, this phrase echoed worldwide. Serving as a beacon of unity for some and a hollow slogan for others. It was a year that forced us to take a global time-out, reassess our connections, and consider our contributions to society.

Fast-forward to today and we are on the brink of political and technological revolutions. The masses want to be heard, while the people in charge are forcing their old agendas. All while the boon of robotics and AI knocks at our doors. Tech giants promise a utopia where the daily grind will be obsolete, while the masses struggle to understand how they'll survive without employment.

The question that looms is what will be lost by embracing this technology? What will we miss out on if we don't embrace it at all?

Through the whiplash of "getting back to normal" parallelled with a utopian future...it's understandable that people are feeling divided. Many are eager to shut themselves away and veg out on fast media.

"SURVIVORS DON'T DIE" dives into these themes against the backdrop of a corporate city that rose to power by working together. The series challenges viewers to consider whether an advanced society both technologically and socially can truly remain united in adversity. It questions the durability of a society that lifts up the individual while still maintaining a sense of community. Probing the depths of human identity in the process.

Mixing found family themes with a reflective tone, "SURVIVORS DON'T DIE" navigates the murky waters between technological advancement and the power of human connection. It's a narrative that asks us to consider what the future holds and whether the dream of a perfect society is just that —a dream.

THE STORY

In 2123, the corporate city of Nuvitta is still battling the deadly X80 pandemic. Zombies roam the streets, making it more difficult to gather supplies. Five heroes bunkered down in the southern part of the city are on a mission to find others like them.

At the start, the crew is led by the strategic Oli Callahan, a no-nonsense woman with a nose for strategy and survival. She's employed tech genius Yuki Russo and her android brother, Tim, to fix the city's communication network. Led by the belief that they'll have power in numbers, they hope to make contact before their supplies run out. Unfortunately, the cautious Dr. Zola Bulle, and the robust Ji Hardy, have low expectations the plan will work in their favor.

When they get word of a possible survivor, they take to the streets to bolster their ranks. On their journey, they find themselves ambushed by a zombie horde. In a desperate attempt to escape, they come face to face with something even worse - Hive Bees! These security drones are known to abduct survivors and take them to an unknown fate.

However, when they wake up in The Sanctuary District, our crew discovers a familiar society of human decency. A zombie-free utopia that claims to have a cure, as long as civilians participate in a medical and spiritual 7-Step Program.

The crew attempts to settle in, only to find that Yuki's determination to reunite with her android brother, Tim, stirs up some unexpected turmoil. Meanwhile, Zola begins to notice medical anomalies within his patients, hinting at a darker truth. While Ji and Oli encounter the militarized side of enforcing the Sanctuary rules. All the while, Tim, fights the hordes beyond the Hive wall to reunite with his only remaining family.

As they grapple with staying safe or taking their chances, they're introduced to the sinister visions of the future by Nuvitta's CEO, Amala Von Brandt. She envisions a future where humanity undergoes a biological revolution. Under the guise of The Program, the corporation is experimenting on willing test subjects. They're eager to redefine what it means to be human.

As secrets are discovered, our survivors make alliances with unexpected rebel groups both in and out of The Sanctuary District. Together, they fight against the tyrannical rule within the walls of the corporate fortress.

This season of "SURVIVORS DON'T DIE" promises a danger-filled journey of discovery and a quest for autonomy. Exploring betrayals, alliances, and an unyielding human spirit, this story explores the courage and the price of a technological utopia. Viewers will be left to ponder: Can you survive a world without a promise of tomorrow? Are you willing to do what it takes to ensure humanity lives another day?

THE CITY

Nuvitta, founded by web3 moguls in 2068, is a pioneering example of a privatized real estate venture. For the last 55 years, it has leveraged technology to enhance human existence. The city once boasted advanced infrastructure, renewable energy sources, cutting-edge healthcare, and unique forms of transportation. It had set a gold standard for modern urban living.

A key innovation was using a Universal Basic Income (UBI) program. This ensured all citizens had their basic needs of food, housing, and water met. This improved mental and physical well-being for all citizens, fueling rapid technological and social innovations.

Two years after the city became ground zero for The X80 Infection, the streets are no longer safe. Only 1% of 3 million citizens fight to survive.

Hordes of undead are attracted to sound and movement. Prowling the streets for their next meal. Survivors have ditched their automatic weapons and madk do with silent alternatives to protect themselves.

Worst of all, Nuvitta was known for the largest population of augmented citizens before the infection. With a community of 600k augmented individuals, it's believed a majority of them are now Zomborgs. These zombies have implanted technology in their bodies that allows them to run faster, hear better, bite harder, and hunt with a precision that has never been seen in the horror genre.

As survivors become far and few between, a large wall separates the city's eastern border. Survivors have called this place THE HIVE. But little do they know, beyond this wall is a sanctuary trying to return to the community Nuvitta once nurtured.

THE INFECTION

In 2121, a meteoroid the size of a basketball landed in a convenience shop in the northern district of Brightwell - releasing a fungal spore into the air. This alien spore found that humans were a prime host for its reproduction process. The disease was originally coined Disseminated X80 Mucormycosis. It was later shortened to The X80 infection.

There are three stages of infection.

Stage 1: Dormant Airborne Exposure
Because the fungal spore is delivered through the air, it is believed that the entire population of Nuvitta has been infected. The mold can remain dormant in the body's bloodstream for an undetermined number of years. People rarely have any side effects.

Stage 2: Extreme Serotonin Exposure
When X80 is exposed to large doses of serotonin, as seen when the host body dies - the buildup of mold begins an unprecedented growth period. This chemical reaction can take up to 36-hrs. The fungus can then reanimate and control the host body.

To keep the host functioning, however, the mutated fungus must consume living flesh. This can cause hosts to perform violent acts they may not have been capable of performing before the mutation.

This effect can also be induced by certain antidepressants.

It is recommended that all bodies upon natural death be burned before the mutation can take hold.

Stage 3: Dormant Contact with a Mutated Strain
When hosts with a dormant version of X80 are exposed to a mutated strain through the exchange of a bite or direct contact with mutated blood, they will experience a more rapid-fire growth stage. This growth period can take anywhere from 30 seconds to 1hr to complete.

Once turned, hosts will experience the same desires for living flesh and perform violent acts to feed the mutated infection within their bodies.

Can zombies be cured? There is some debate as to whether the mutation of the fungal spore can be removed/healed. Many believe that the only cure is a bullet to the head.

NUVITTA
1. OLD TOWN
2. CAMBRIA
3. SALT TOWN
4. HARLEY BAY
5. DOGHILL
6. BRIGHTWELL
7. SOUTHGATE
8. DARKYARD
9. THE SANCTUARY

NUVITTA DISTRICTS

1. OLD TOWN - Historical District - Located at the center of the city, this is where the original buildings were built and later converted into the political square. Many city functions, celebrations, and announcements took place here.

2. CAMBRIA - Business District - State-of-the-art high-rises and office buildings tower over the city from Cambria. This is where many innovators, financiers, artists, and technology scientists worked.

3. SALT TOWN - Residential & Educational District - This residential and educational district had middle-class housing. The schools in this district serviced everyone in the city. Hosting preschool to college, most civilians were comfortable in this part of town.

4. HARLEY BAY - Transportation District - The location of Nuvitta's port patrol, this district used to service sailors and their families. Those who lived in this district were usually "lower-middle class" and tied to jobs of service (police, firefighter, military, etc.)

5. DOGHILL - Entertainment District in Nuvitta - Doghill was best known for its great nightlife, entertainment venues, and some of the best restaurants in the world. Those who lived in this area were mostly single, upper-middle-class citizens.

6. BRIGHTWELL - Upper-Class District - This district was where the majority of the wealthiest Nuvitta residents lived. McMansions, family-focused neighborhoods, and well-maintained parks. This is where you wanted to raise children and where you looked forward to growing old.

7. SOUTHGATE - Low-Income District - This district was a residential district where low-income and affordable housing was built. It included several parks and agricultural towers. Many who lived and worked here were food- and customer-service technicians or lived exclusively on UBI with no additional credits.

8. DARKYARD - Network District - This district is where those who worked for the Nuvitta Network lived and worked. This included technicians, developers, and tech nerds. It is where our heroes set up their bunker for the last few years.

9. THE SANCTUARY - Sanctuary District - Six months after the pandemic annihilated the Nuvitta public, a large WALL was 3D-printed around a small section of Salt Town. Survivors were unaware of who was behind the structure but made note of the Bee-like drones that patrolled it. Anyone who got too close to the wall was never seen again. It is known by many as, The Hive.

THE EPISODES

SURVIVORS DON'T DIE will launch with a 7-episode exploration into the world and its dangers. Each episode will be modeled after a step in "The Program," an indoctrination process for new survivors in the Sanctuary District. Each episode will explore various themes and concepts that define humanity.

Episode 1: Introduction

Yuki and a group of survivors set out on a mission to find others like them, but get more than they bargained for when security drones abduct them. Introduced to The Sanctuary District, our heroes must adjust to life in a civilized community that seems too good to be true. When Tim is left behind, he attempts to rescue his friends at a grievous cost.

Episode 2: Education

As the survivors undergo an orientation about The Program, they learn about the mysterious process that could save humanity. Their assimilation into The Sanctuary District comes with odd observations and the attraction of community members they aren't certain they can trust. Meanwhile, Tim attempts a second rescue mission with the aid of a large Zombie Horde.

Episode 3: Community

Tim breaks into the Sanctuary District with the help of a Zomborg. Our survivors are tested on their worthiness to remain in The Sanctuary District. These tests reveal the true nature of the community's intention, forcing our heroes to question their loyalties and desire for survival.

Episode 4: Audit

Forced to participate in the Audit, our crew faces their past and reveals to the Nuvitta Corporation just how useful they will be to the survival of humanity. Just as they battle with the not-so-voluntary circumstances of their new home, our heroes will discover that others want to leave The Sanctuary District too.

Episode 5: Commitment

During our crew's attempt to flee their new home, they unveil Nuvitta's dark secrets. Their commitment to each other forces the hand of the city's CEO to threaten Yuki's only family left. Militarized protocols are put in place to keep the population under control. The City CEO is determined to stamp out any form of insurgence.

Episode 6: Improvement

As our group of survivors rebels against Nuvitta's oppressive regime, they experience tense confrontations with community leaders. Meanwhile, Tim arrives with a stronger army and a "winner takes all" focus to save his family.

Episode 7: Verification

The survivors face their final challenge as Yuki undergoes the cure against her will. The survivors must confront their deepest fears and fight for their survival in a race against time. Will they succeed in breaking free from Nuvitta's grasp and find a way to save humanity?

GENRE & TONE

SURVIVORS DON'T DIE will combine sci-fi and horror classics in a way both genres have yet to experience.

Our characters will entertain fan-favorite archetypes of Found Family Teams, Corporate Overlords, Mad Scientists, Political Rebels, and Judas-Level-Traitors, each trying to survive a unique zombie apocalypse littered with cyborg zombies.

Visually we want to play with high-contrast imagery to portray the differences in Nuvitta and The Sanctuary District. While Nuvitta embraces rigid skyscrapers, and eco-friendly buildings, the rot and decay of the X80 infection has taken the shine out of the once flourishing city. Now its rusty parts cope with darker tones, deeper shadows, and starker visuals.

Meanwhile, The Sanctuary District will be bright, sunny, and littered with joy and color. An obnoxiously beautiful and serene calm will be associated with this living space. It will be a stark division from the city beyond their walls. It will also make our character's decision to stay or go that much more difficult.

This visual dichotomy not only enhances the narrative tension but also deepens the thematic exploration of dystopia versus utopia. Offering viewers a vivid representation of the series' underlying conflicts.

With characters labeled with a color and a number to designate their "progress" in "The Program," we'll be able to play with the colored tones of each stage per episode. This will allow the audience to experience their own form of cult-like ascension to higher ranks.

This innovative approach to visual storytelling will engage the audience in a multisensory experience, mirroring the characters' journey through The Program. By combining the beauty of both the sci-fi and horror genres, we'll be able to portray the world of SURVIVORS DON'T DIE in a way that has never been seen before.

THE CREW

YUKI RUSSO

June 7, 2110	13
DATE OF BIRTH	**AGE**
Level 13	Engineer Training
EDUCATION	**FOCUS**
School Training (NAT Score Age Sufficient)	
OCCUPATIONAL ASSIGNMENT	
Darkyard	"Kid" or "Yuke"
RESIDENCE	**KNOWN ALIAS**
N/A	Limited/Underage
POLITICS	**SOCIAL CIRCLE**

ADDITIONAL SURVEILLANCE NOTES

Nuvitta Aptitude Test returned a Level 18 Module recommendation. Given her 2-year absence from the system. It is recommended she be placed in the age-appropriate Level 13.

PERSONALITY NOTES:

Observations of Yuki Russo from the age of 5 years old suggest that she prides herself on her individuality. She enjoys praise and succeeding in her focused tasks. She is motivated and exhibits an unshakable work ethic. However, her lack of respect for authority has required repeat communications training since she began schooling. Despite this, her personality makes her well-liked among her peers, though there are concerns about her potentially being a bad influence on younger trainees.

MAIN TRAITS: Motivated, Stubborn, Opinionated, Loyal, Social   **MBTI:** INFP-T   **ENNEAGRAM:** 4

PUBLIC LIKES	PUBLIC DISLIKES	FAMILY
- Video Games	- Card Games	Mother - Hanna Russo
- Animals	- Wet Socks	Deceased at 36 - Metro Architect
- Licorice	- Black Licorice	
- Technology	- Country Music	Father - Leonardo Russo
- Winning Awards	- Birds	Deceased at 37 - Network Developer
- Humor	- Medical Treatments	
- Praise	- Authority	Brother - Genji Ruso
		Deceased at 16 - Historian Trainee

PRODUCTION NOTES:

Throughout the series, Yuki Russo will be one of the main characters through which the audience explores the world of Zomborgs. The audience will witness her bonds with her crewmates, her resentment toward Nuvitta's authority, her struggles with the shifting hierarchy, and her confusion when she encounters puppy love for the first time.

Yuki's youthful energy, headstrong personality, and ability to keep up with the adults in her life will help her survive the tribulations she will face. Exploring her pandemic traumas and the demand for her to grow up quickly will provide insights into how young people can adapt differently than adults in similar situations.

OLIVIA CALLAHAN

April 27, 2080	43
DATE OF BIRTH	**AGE**
Level 24	Military Strategy
EDUCATION	**FOCUS**
Android Unit Leader | Sanctuary Security Patrol	
OCCUPATIONAL ASSIGNMENT	
Salt Town	"Oli" or "Ols"
RESIDENCE	**KNOWN ALIAS**
Sideliner	Occupational
POLITICS	**SOCIAL CIRCLE**

ADDITIONAL SURVEILLANCE NOTES

Worked as an Android Unit Leader, known by superiors as a hard worker and capable of completing tasks. Personality was known to be reliable and generally easy to work with. Reassignment to Sanctuary Security Patrol is recommended.

PERSONALITY NOTES:

Security Specialist Oli Callahan has proven time and again that her ability to accomplish goals with the least amount of damage is above average. Her logical thinking and decisiveness is a major asset to any leadership role she naturally takes on. She's known amongst her peers as an individual who will speak honestly and does not mince words. Her passionate desire for equality and understanding of the status quo make her an ideal candidate for negotiating compromises between workers and management.

MAIN TRAITS: Self-Reliant, Domineering, Risk-Taker, Protective   **MBTI:** ESTJ-T   **ENNEAGRAM:** 8

PUBLIC LIKES	PUBLIC DISLIKES	FAMILY
- European Football - Dancing - Strawberry Hard Candy - Health & Fitness - Accomplishing Goals - Honesty - Strategic Planning	- Loud Music - Messy Environments - Tea Is For The Weak - Prejudiced Management - Being Challenged - Insubordination - Slackers	Wife - Rachel Callahan Missing at age 43 - Physical Therapist Lead Son - Marcus Callahan Deceased at age 12 - Medical Trainee Daughter - Abigail Callahan Missing at age 6 - Level 6 Trainee

PRODUCTION NOTES:

Oli Callahan will fill multiple social roles within the series. Her goal to keep those she can safe will be a driving force against the guilt of losing her family. She is tough, pragmatic, and focused on survival. Her belief in strength in numbers will be challenged while they adapt to living within The Sanctuary District.

With her blunt tone of conversation and overprotective nature, Oli's journey throughout the series represents the struggle between pragmatism and idealism. She will experience moments of confrontation, vulnerability, and regret. As well as be put in positions where her skills in lowering collateral damage and delegating tasks to accomplish large goals can be realized.

JI HARDY

Feb 25, 2071	52
DATE OF BIRTH	**AGE**
Level 20	Security Patrol
EDUCATION	**FOCUS**

Former CFO Security | Resigned Patrol Service
OCCUPATIONAL ASSIGNMENT

Doghill	N/A
RESIDENCE	**KNOWN ALIAS**
Nuvitta	Residential Acquaintances
POLITICS	**SOCIAL CIRCLE**

ADDITIONAL SURVEILLANCE NOTES

A low-ranked security member under Nuvitta's former CFO, Leonard Hastings. While not considered for advancement, he provides effective physical security when needed. He is a useful candidate for the Residential Patrol role.

PERSONALITY NOTES:

Observations of Ji Hardy suggest that he takes pride in his toughness and enjoys projecting an intimidating persona. Colleagues have reported that he is outspoken, wears his heart on his sleeve, and can be easily excited when drinking or smoking. His work ethic has been described as "gruff but useful," and he has had trouble advancing in his career. While he may have a morally-gray approach, he has not acted on any illegal precedent. His primal personality and comedic timing make him well-liked and tolerated by those in his inner circle.

MAIN TRAITS: Gruff, Independent, Impassioned, Risk-Averse   **MBTI:** ENFP-T   **ENNEAGRAM:** 7

PUBLIC LIKES	PUBLIC DISLIKES	FAMILY
- Beer & Smokes - Attractive People - Gummy Bears - Working Out - Cooking - Fucking - Sleeping	- Classical Music - Sitting with his back to the door - Fish and Sushi - Being told what to do - Decaf coffee - People who talk too much - Looking weak	Mother - Nalani Hardy Deceased at 76 - Executive Banquet Chef Father - Andre Hardy Deceased at 77 - Heavy Equipment Operator Ex-Wife - Janice Kekoa 48 years old - Farm Technician

PRODUCTION NOTES:

Ji Hardy will serve as the muscle of the crew throughout the series. His loyalty to the group will create dramatic and comedic situations as they navigate their new world together. He will assume the role of a protective uncle. While also providing a blunt and outspoken personality that often says what everyone is thinking.

Ji's character highlights the issues of "us vs. them" thinking patterns and the challenges of overcoming divisions in a zombie-infested world. He will go through moments of confusion, anger, and forgiveness. His physical strength will be called upon in situations where confrontation is necessary.

ZOLA BULLE

Oct 10, 2085	38
DATE OF BIRTH	**AGE**
Level 27	General Surgery
EDUCATION	**FOCUS**

Emergency Surgeon | Sanctuary General Practitioner
OCCUPATIONAL ASSIGNMENT

Brightwell	"Zo"
RESIDENCE	**KNOWN ALIAS**
Netural	Occupational
POLITICS	**SOCIAL CIRCLE**

ADDITIONAL SURVEILLANCE NOTES

Served as a top emergency physician at Nuvitta General for 11 years, Zola Bulle's patient survival rating surpasses the national average. He was on track to become a Nuvitta General Board Member. Reassignment to the Sanctuary Hospital asap.

PERSONALITY NOTES:

Observations of Zola Bulle would suggest that he is someone who prides himself on his level-headed leadership style. He can de-escalate issues with leaders quickly and efficiently. He is motivated by his observational instincts and calming personality. Peers tend to trust him quickly. While he respects authority, he can be easily influenced and open to other belief systems. Zola's emotionally mature personality makes him a leader who excels at teamwork. He serves as an excellent role model for younger trainees and aspiring caregivers.

MAIN TRAITS: Focused, Empathetic, Fair, Balanced, Social   **MBTI:** INFP-A   **ENNEAGRAM:** 9

PUBLIC LIKES

- Gardening
- Nice things
- Hot Meals
- Investing
- Video Games
- Meditation
- Home Parties

PUBLIC DISLIKES

- Arguments
- Energy Vampires
- Chocolate
- Heavy Metal
- Wasps
- Dentists
- Bullies

FAMILY

Mother - Zuri Bulle
Deceased at 57 - Assistant Professor

Father - Joon Bulle
Deceased at 60 - NATO Communications Officer

Spouse - Sandy Bulle
Deceased at 33 - Online Entrepreneur

PRODUCTION NOTES:

Dr. Zola Bulle will serve as the audience's guide into the underground operations of the Sanctuary District throughout the series. We will witness his mediation skills with his crewmates and his ability to gain the trust of Sanctuary residents. He will grapple with the dilemma of whom to trust.

Zola's composed demeanor, emotional maturity, and talent for maintaining a calm environment will serve as a guiding light for the other crew members. His struggles with moral dilemmas and the need to protect himself and his fellow survivors will generate dramatic tension throughout the series.

TIM RUSSO

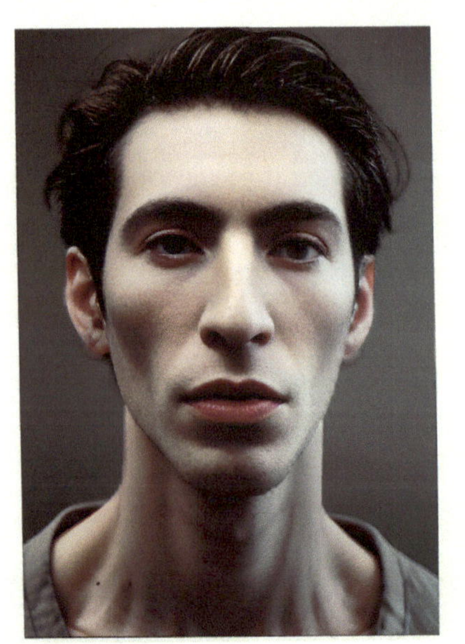

Feb 1, 2116 (Activation Date)

DATE OF BIRTH

7

AGE

N/A

EDUCATION

Android Service

FOCUS

Provide collaborative assistance to Russo Family.

OCCUPATIONAL ASSIGNMENT

Darkyard

RESIDENCE

N/A

KNOWN ALIAS

N/A

POLITICS

Russo Family

SOCIAL CIRCLE

ADDITIONAL SURVEILLANCE NOTES

Purchased by the Russo family in 2116 for assistance in childcare, household tasks, and occupational assistance. This mycelium unit was approved for import by The Nuvitta Corporation Android Program. Licenses are renewed yearly.

PERSONALITY NOTES:

Base training of this unit includes a family imprint system, a friendly personality protocol, and an emphasis on protecting underaged members of the assigned family. It is understood that yearly upgrades made to the system will document trained data that can be mistaken for personality. As of the last upgrade in 2120, this unit has learned the importance of family, optimism, and navigation. Used mainly by Genji and Yuki Russo for education, this unit has been upgraded with historical references to media, pop culture, and landmark events. Additional upgrades include mechanical and network engineering.

MAIN TRAITS: Optimistic, Friendly, Smart, Loyal   **MBTI:** INTJ-A   **ENNEAGRAM:** 5

PUBLIC LIKES	PUBLIC DISLIKES	FAMILY
None Available	None Available	Russo Family Property

PRODUCTION NOTES:

Tim's role within the series will embody all the positive traits we think of when being human. An android designed to be as human as possible, Tim will provide us with a reflection of our own loyalty, dedication, and love within the story. His loyalty and desperation to return to Yuki will place him in dangerous Zombie infested streets beyond the Sanctuary wall.

He is a representation of how emotionally connected humans can get to their personal technology. Tim will provide us with opportunities to explore what it really means to live and exist in an era of Artificial Intelligence once it becomes normal.

AMALA VON BRANDT

Jan 27, 2058	65
DATE OF BIRTH	**AGE**
MS Harvard University	Crisis Leadership
EDUCATION	**FOCUS**
Chief Executive Officer of Nuvitta Co.	
OCCUPATIONAL ASSIGNMENT	
Cambria	"Ama"
RESIDENCE	**KNOWN ALIAS**
Nuvitta Co.	N/A
POLITICS	**SOCIAL CIRCLE**

ADDITIONAL SURVEILLANCE NOTES

Appointed as the Nuvitta CEO in 2100 at the age of 42. Prior to her appointment, she served as Nuvitta's Crisis Management Director for 10 years. Her exceptional leadership has significantly improved Nuvitta's quality of life and stock prices.

PERSONALITY NOTES:

Amala Von Brandt has built a successful career based on her ability to excel in any situation. Her meticulous attention to detail, aptitude for forecasting outcomes, understanding of multiple perspectives, and natural talent for data analysis make her an invaluable asset to the Nuvitta Corporation. Known for her fairness, focus, and diligence, she has the ability to rally others to support her causes, projects, and beliefs. She has consistently demonstrated her leadership by spearheading innovative initiatives within the community to address large-scale issues and internal conflicts.

MAIN TRAITS: Charming, Charismatic, Impatient, Manipulative   **MBTI:** INFJ-T   **ENNEAGRAM:** 1

PUBLIC LIKES

- Money
- Power
- Tennis
- Fine Wines
- Modern Art
- Cheese Boards
- Nootropics

PUBLIC DISLIKES

- Disobedience
- Being Doubted
- Incompetence
- Red Meat
- Animals
- Litter Bugs
- The Unknown

FAMILY

Personal information for CEO's is highly classified for safety protocols.

PRODUCTION NOTES:

Amala Von Brandt will serve as the primary antagonist in our series. She will utilize The Program to conduct her nefarious experiments and unravel the mysteries of human nature. Her personality will mislead our heroes, gaining the trust of certain members, manipulating their motivations, and undermining their unity to bend them to her will.

Her desire to control the population within The Sanctuary District for the supposed betterment of all will propagate the message of, "We are all in this together." However, her understanding of human psychology, expertise in crisis management, and her mission to save the human race at any cost will ultimately put her at odds with the ethical and moral values she claims to hold dear.

WHAT NEXT?

You just started a journey, my friend. Now, the question on both our minds should be... will you continue onward?

Is this world worth your brain space?

Or should it be burned as a sacrifice to the story goblins so your brain can be wiped clean of the memories?

We're on a mission to become the best storytellers on the damn planet.

Our goal is to tell stories other people want to see. But we won't know if others want more unless you tell us.

If you're interested in giving feedback or want the next episode you can scratch that itch at;

OHHEYVOID.COM

What you say may just decide whether this project gets made into your next favorite series.

Episode #2
Episode #1
F.Disode #3
F.Diso.
Episode #6

CREDITS

Created by:
Amber Wilkinson & Jayson Wall

All images were created with synthography, 3D, and
other CGI workflows. For more information on our
creative process visit OhHeyVoid.com.

Special Thanks:
The Wilkinson Family
Rolayne Martin
The Pack

Thank You!

We're a two-person team using all the new tech to get better at storytelling. Whenever someone takes the time to read what we create, it means the world to us. This project has been so much fun, and we hope you enjoyed it as much as we have.

If you're interested in learning more about the SURVIVORS DON'T DIE PROJECT visit our website for updates, exclusive releases, and more.

OHHEYVOID.com

Oh Hey
VOID!